Forgiveness

THE QUEST FOR HEALING YOUR HEART

SHARETTA DONALSON

Printed in the United States of America

ISBN 13: 978-0-9991203-0-9

DEDICATION

This book is dedicated to victims of abuse who are afraid, ashamed, and voiceless and to anyone struggling to forgive and move forward.

ACKNOWLEDGMENTS

I would like to thank my husband, Anderson, who has wiped my tears and supported me through this process. I would also like to thank my children who always encourage me to expand my horizon. Your sacrifices will never go unnoticed.

To my parents who gave me a foundation in forgiveness to build upon. I can always hear my mother saying, "Don't treat people the way they treat you." That was her version of 1 Peter 3:9 which says, *"Don't repay evil with evil or insult with insult……"*

To my pastor and first lady who have always given me truth, love, and hope.

To my family and friends, thanks for being sounding boards and prayer partners.

To Tamika L. Sims, thanks for coaching me through this process. As I write I can hear you say, *"Honey, I'm not into mediocrity."*

And to Dr. Rose Wiley-Jackson, my high school English and Literature instructor who taught me two hours a day for two years, thanks for requiring excellence in writing from me. You deposited more into me pertaining to writing than anyone ever could.

Table of Contents

Introduction

I was sexually abused nearly thirty years ago, but the memories are forever etched in my mind. I can remember the exact day it started. In those days, we lived on a narrow road in Canton, Mississippi, a small rural town. My grandmother was a prominent landowner and many of our family members lived on that land. Big family shindigs were common for us. We could sit around for hours eating and laughing. The adults would spark up card games on the picnic tables while the children played sporting games, most of which we made up. Those days were glorious. However, there was evil lurking underneath the laughter that I was not aware of.

The innocence of my childhood came to a screeching halt, the day I was awakened by violating sexual touches. I thought I was home alone. I had stayed home from school because I felt ill and had a sore throat, which would be later diagnosed as mumps. As I became more awakened and realized I was not in a dream, I immediately became paralyzed with fear. I could not see who was touching me because my back was turned. But when I finally came face to face with my attacker, I was shocked to see my father. My daddy, the shrewd disciplinarian, had turned from protector to perpetrator. I was accustomed to getting old-fashioned whippings at his hands that sometimes required first-aid afterwards, but this was more vile. This was day one, the beginning of a dark era. He was tearfully apologetic and admitted himself into a mental institution that same day. I thought that this would be a one-time occurrence, but once he returned home, the abuse continued. It was repetitive and binding, similar to that of sex slavery.

I told someone that first day, but was instructed to never tell anyone else what happened. The person that I thought would rescue me, told me that in order to protect my mother's heart, I needed to take this secret to the grave with me. I was left alone to suffer in silence. From that moment on, I quickly became accustomed to how sounds could become muffled when ears are filled with tears. Most sexual crimes committed against minors are at the hands of someone they know; family members, close family friends, or church members. It was no different with me. Someone that I looked to for love and protection had opened a wicked,

2

vile, and sadistic Pandora's box and unleashed upon me the worse violation

of love and protection that I have ever encountered.

FORGIVENESS

vile, and sadistic Pandora's box and unleashed upon me the worse violation

of love and protection that I have ever encountered.

FORGIVENESS

CHAPTER ONE

The Entrance of Fear

The backdrop of my story started in the spring of 1981. I was awakened by screams and an aggressively loud voice. The voices I heard were my parents'. I became alert then because I had not seen any violence between them before. My father was dragging my mother through our hallway. My mother started to scream out to me to take the kids and run out the back door. I was only seven years old at the time and the oldest of the three siblings that had been born. My other siblings were five years old and the baby was less than six months of age. Whenever my mother screamed for me to run, my father would threaten to kill my mother if I did. At seven years old, I had to make the decision to save my mother's life or to try to preserve my own and that of my sisters. I opted to stay. Before the night ended, my mother found a large plumber's wrench and struck my father on the head. We made it out that night and went next door to his mother's house and summon for more help. As a child, I heard many rumors of what triggered my father's rage that night. The older people called it a "nervous breakdown," while others say someone had put "something" in his drink. I did not understand the half of what was said, but I knew I was scared and traumatized.

The roller coaster ride of my father being in and out of mental hospitals had officially begun. He would get better and regress. We started sleeping in clothes because we were unsure of when we would have to run out of the house to safety in the middle of the night. The best times were when he was in the hospital or when we were allowed to stay at our grandmother's house. We could relax and let our guards down.

He could come home for the weekends during some of his hospital stays. We had to prepare our homes to receive him by clearing out anything that could be used as a weapon against us or himself. On one weekend pass, he used a credit card to get in a locked closet where the guns were located in his mother's house. We literally had to run for our lives in the middle of the day. Adults and children took cover to preserve their lives. My father eventually suffered a self-inflicted, nonfatal gunshot wound to his chest. This solidified my fear of him and that fear set the stage for the abuse. I literally went from wearing clothes to bed in case I had to run for my life, to wearing clothes to bed to discourage his sexual advances.

The clothes were not effective to keep him from having sex with me. No matter how many clothes I had on, how asleep I pretended to be, or how I tried to resist, he was determined to fulfill his lustful desires when he wanted to. Not only was I afraid and instructed not to tell, he put enmity between my mother and I by speaking against her instructions to me. He would tell me that she was too hard on me and that she fussed at me too much. This was the old divide and conquer technique.

During the abuse, my father began pastoring a church. The abuse did not stop even then. In a desperate plea, I showed him a Scripture where certain sexual acts were unlawful. I thought that if I showed him proof that sex with his daughter was wrong from the book he preached from, he would have a change of heart. Instead, I was treated like his in-house mistress. I could not speak to male classmates if he was present. He would watch me through the rearview mirror of the car when the family was riding. If I turned my head to look out of the window, I was questioned about it when he got me alone. He wanted to make sure that I was not watching any boys. I was under constant observation in his presence.

The abuse rocked me to my very core. He eventually impregnated me. I knew nothing about missed periods being an indicator of pregnancy. I was only in the tenth grade in the late 80s. My father told my mother and blamed the pregnancy on someone that had never touched or even kissed me. I was soon taken to an obstetrician for my first examination. The doctor who examined attempted to make a joke about the pregnancy. He said to his assistant that it seemed someone had been sneaking under the bleachers with the boys at the football games. As he chuckled, I wished that he really knew what happened. I never saw him again because the obvious response to this incestuous pregnancy was an abortion. First I was taken to abortion clinic here in Mississippi. My head was covered as I walked through protesters who tried to shove pictures of dismembered babies in my face. I did not have an abortion that day. After an ultrasound, where I saw a moving baby, it was revealed that the baby was past the allowed gestational age to have an abortion in the state of Mississippi. I was then taken to Metairie, Louisiana to have this procedure performed to remove this fully formed baby.

I was alone with my father on this trip. We had to stay the night in a hotel. I was more afraid of what he could do to me without the restraints of being in the home with the whole family than the abortion itself. The first day at the clinic, the doctor performed a portion of the procedure and informed me that I could not engage in any sexual activity that night. I was relieved that I could sleep peaceably that night. I knew that I wouldn't be pulled from the bed. I knew that we could eat dinner and have a normal night alone almost like a father and daughter, except for the fact that I had his baby inside of me. After the abortion, we came back to Mississippi and I slept all the way.

From the time of the abortion on, my life started taking detours that I never would have imagined. The fear I had for my father started to decrease. I thought, "What more can he do to me besides kill me?" I wanted to hurt people because I was hurt and abuse people because I was abused. Although it was wrong, I was sucked into a vicious cycle. At times, I was a shell with no insides similar to a decaying turtle. Other times I was totally mushy similar to that of a slug. I was unknowingly incomplete, broken, and imbalanced searching for something to erase my history and let me live anew. I wondered who knew? Whenever I heard someone reference secrets and having skeleton's in one's closet, my mind immediately went to those countless nights of abuse, feeling as if I did something to deserve it. I relived those nights, and even some days, a million times over. These memories nearly robbed me of my life, my liberty, and my pursuit of happiness.

CHAPTER TWO

Failed Relationships

In my brokenness, I began to search for completeness and happiness in other people. I became friends with a guy who eventually became my high school sweetheart. He started visiting me in my home. One day as we played in the yard, my father watched us through the bushes across the road. When the gentleman left and my father could speak to me alone, I was questioned severely about that, but I had lost all respect for him and at that point, I really did not care. I continued my relationship with that gentleman and he eventually became my best friend and refuge from the madness. We became romantically involved. I eventually got pregnant and married him before I graduated from high school. His mother was adamant about us raising our child in a two-parent home and I was immediately sold on the idea because I wanted to escape my current living conditions.

Our marriage barely survived two years, mainly because I could not cope with my past effectively. We were two great people but we were too young and he was no match for the demons that I had been exposed to. He was away from home hanging with the guys most nights and I started seeing someone else. We eventually went our separate ways. I moved back home because I had no choice. I was awakened one night by a hand on my chest and my father standing over me, I moved out the next day and I started living with a young man that I started seeing while I was married.

In 1994, I was 19 years old, and pregnant with a third child by a third person. Throughout that relationship, I was the most unstable ever. I was rebellious and easily angered. After the baby was born, I would have emotional meltdowns and break dishes. I would throw knives at my boyfriend and throw his clothes out of the apartment. I would put him out and take him in again. In September of 1995, he was involved in a horrible car accident where one of his friends died on the scene. It was no longer fun and games as he lay in the Intensive Care Unit with machines and tubes everywhere. I was emotionally crushed. For the first time in a long while, I experienced a merger of my hardcore outer shell and my mushy, childlike insides.

I never had the opportunity to apologize. This time I needed forgiveness, but couldn't ask for it. Eventually he died because of the trauma inflicted to his internal organs. During his hospitalization, I slowed down and realized that I needed to change some things about me. I was determined to get on a road to progression. One of the hardest things to do on the road to progression was to camp out at forgiveness. I loved people the best I knew how, but the day they buried my child's father, something changed internally and I became more intentional and deliberate about how I treated and loved people.

The newfound love quest only confirmed to me that I needed to begin at the root of my bitterness. I needed to forgive the person who sexually abused me. Despite how ugly and unnatural it was, I needed to do what I considered to be "my part" in the situation. I forgave him for me.

I still love my father. Our relationship is nothing like what I see with other adult daughters and their fathers, but I manage to live on despite that void that I feel sometimes. There have been times when I thought I was emotionally healed only to realize that the wound was only scabbed over, but there was still underlying irritation. Once the proverbial scab was removed, the healing process continued or restarted. I can remember sitting in a women's conference while the minister taught on the Biblical story of Tamar of the Old Testament and how she felt when her brother raped her. The scab came off for me again. I realized there were more areas that I needed to work on so that I could operate in completeness. I allowed the Counselor and Great Physician to work on me and I became even more determined not to live fractured in my emotions.

I wanted to render the ugly monster of abuse helpless and ineffective in my life and in the lives of other survivors. I came to the realization that I was indeed a survivor. No counselor could empower me to overcome the attacks of the spirit of perversion like the Holy Spirit did. The times that I tried to survive apart from the Holy Spirit, I failed miserably. I lived in shame, fear, and at times loneliness even while being surrounded by a room of people. I could not watch television shows about sexual abuse. I would spark a random conversation with whomever I was watching it with to silence the message of abuse awareness. I did not want the awareness. I thought surely everyone would blame me as if I would dare be so bold as to try and seduce my own father.

I remember the day I felt an unction of Holy Spirit to tell my current husband. I knew that the Lord was preparing me for something greater, something that could possibly help other survivors. Fear rose in me like an erupting volcano just as the day the abuse started. I wanted to say it verbally, but couldn't. I was so afraid he would abandon me and slander my name across town. I opted to write him a letter. We have managed to be married 16 years now and have added three more children to the two I had before we met. God started advancing us in stages.

We started attending church together. The more I learned about forgiveness and the love of God, the more I could manage my emotions. As I learned how to control myself, I could pursue a career. While a senior in high school, I had my first child, got married, and moved away to a neighboring county. I continued and graduated from high school with honors, but I had worked in the fast food industry for most of the time since high school. I tried college several times for short periods, but I could not seem to focus. I forfeited a full academic scholarship and came back home to work in fast food.

FORGIVENESS

Eventually, through the twists and turns of life, I was able to go back to nursing school in 1999, completing a practical nursing program. I returned to school again in 2006 and completed a Registered Nurse program with an Associate's Degree. In 2016, I completed my bachelor's degree in Nursing. I have been gainfully employed in the nursing profession since obtaining my first licensure in 1999.

All of this happened because of my determination to forgive and allow God to fix whatever needed to be fixed in my life and in my relationships. If I was bitter and angry, I could very well be anywhere besides living a productive life. In my career as a nurse, I have seen countless numbers of mentally ill people with histories of some type of abuse. God's mercy empowered me to survive and thrive and prayerfully become a beacon of hope to someone else. I am so earnestly thankful to God and humbled by His mercy to be in this place that I am right now, writing this book to tell other people about the power of forgiveness.

In this book, you will be able to define forgiveness, dispel the myths associated with forgiveness, how to forgive others, how to seek forgiveness, and how to forgive yourself. Join me in prayer as we unleash the ability to forgive in you. Please open your hearts and recite these words out loud in faith.

Father God,

I am asking that the Holy Spirit reveal to me the inner workings of my heart. Expose areas of unforgiveness that I may have. Heal depths of my heart that I may have ignored and restore me that I may be a suitable vessel to help someone else. Equip me with a boldness to do your will and relieve me of any shame as I exchange it for your joy, in Jesus name. Amen.

FORGIVENESS

CHAPTER THREE

Confront to Conquer

I wrote a chilling and vivid account of events in the beginning of this book. They were not the only disappointments that I have experienced nor is this book a full account of all that I have done. I wrote about those that were monumental to me, the things that had a heavy weight and hard impact in my heart. I wish I could say that the journey from living the events to writing the events was an easy one but it certainly wasn't. My journey was marked by detours, potholes, and some roadblocks. One of the pivotal things that occurred on my road to recovery was an overwhelming desire to forgive, heal, and move on to live a normal life. Divorce, sexual assault and abuse, physical and emotional abuse, betrayal, and marriages riddled with infidelities are heavy hitters. They are life-altering events that can have long lasting effects, however, we tap into another level of bravery when we can look life in the face and decide to live on. So many times we have been forced to survive within a box. Society says you can survive, but be quiet about the intricate details. This mindset makes it easy for victims to remain silent and remain hidden. I too was reluctant to share the horrible parts of my life. Exposing my past meant exposing myself. I wanted to get over it; however, there is no getting over until we can confront it.

Bible readers everywhere love the story of David and Goliath. David faced, or confronted his giant while soldiers sat back in fear. David confronted the thing that he thought was a hindrance to what he believed in. We should do the same thing. During the many years that I struggled with whether to come out and confront my past, my fears, and my uncertainties, I was more concerned about everyone's feelings than mine. I became more aware of my emotional needs and I came to grips with the events that set me back in life. I realized that I no longer had to live there. The more the skeletons in my closet rattled, the more I began to set them free. I started inching out of hiding by telling my story to individuals, and then in small meetings, and now to writing this book to empower people who can't seem to confront their past for themselves.

From our pain, we know that there is inspiration and empowerment for other people, but we can't get to that part if we never confront our issues. We can't overcome if we don't confront. We can't be a living testimony if we don't overcome; so, we confront our imperfect pasts to inspire and to motivate others to break free. Moses made it out of Egypt without ever having to be a slave. He had also gotten away with murdering an Egyptian foreman before escaping to safety in the land of Jethro. He had to return to confront Pharaoh, not just for himself, but for others who were oppressed and powerless. Moses' purpose was in his past challenges. Portions of my purpose is also connected to past disappointments. Therefore, we should confront our past and acknowledge our power to overcome. My ability to conquer serves as a reminder of what I can conquer when I tap into the Power Source. There is no way I would have the courage and the ability to conquer without the power of God working in my heart. Past and present victories can set the tone to how you deal with adversities for the rest of your life.

Another reason we confront our past is to free ourselves to live authentically. We no longer must pretend that our disappointments and struggles didn't happen, nor do we have to be ashamed. Living life from a place of authenticity, removes limits and yields another level of transparency. Our pasts no longer should be a hang-up for us. We can live freely without fear keeping us silent. For most of my life, I have lived by the instructions to not tell anyone. Those instructions are now null and void and there is no way I should continue to follow those same instructions. They were soaked in fear and shame; fear of what people might say and pressure to keep reputations clear to avoid shame.

Fear and shame can still and *steal* our voice and keep us from confronting our giants. We predict scenarios and reactions of what might happen in our minds before we even start on our journey. I'm sure David only visualized himself being victorious as he advanced toward Goliath. He knew his past victories of killing the bear and the lion had prepared him for his battle. David trusted God to be his protector and did not allow the fact that he was only a shepherd to stop him even though he was surrounded by suited up soldiers. In my case, there is much to fear: public humiliation, family estrangement, and even retaliation, but no amount of fear is comparable to regaining my self-esteem, confidence, and a voice that has been silenced for nearly three decades. As I became more vocal with my overcoming testimony, I learned that fear had gripped the hearts of people who had an idea of what I was going through. Fear disabled people and kept them from coming to my rescue. When I learned that, I became even more determined to tell my story. I became more determined to sling stones at the antagonizing giant just as David did.

There's no way for me to rewind time and relive my childhood, but I can expose the trauma that I lived through and refuse to be embarrassed. By releasing my shame, I invited people into my healing process. My husband, Anderson, was one of the most important persons that joined me. When I met Anderson, I thought that I was entering this relationship with a clean slate. I wanted to leave all the baggage of previous relationships behind. However, my relationship with my father haunted every relationship I had because I was still dealing with the residue of abuse. When haunting thoughts arose, my job was to acknowledge them and cast them down. I refused to make my husband's life miserable because of another person's failures and mistakes. I also refused to make my children's lives miserable by perpetuating my pain.

I step out as a survivor of incest to de-stigmatize other survivors. My wish is that victims can come out of hiding without fear of being treated like the villain. Victims are not obligated to keep their mouths closed. That battered wife that I heard screaming as I walked past her house, that male that was sexually assaulted by his older cousin; that six-year old girl who was beaten for saying that her grandfather forced himself on her; that 10-

year-old girl who had to be treated repetitively for a sexually transmitted disease, that 13-year-old who had nights of interrupted sleep because she was molested and impregnated by her older brother; and that woman who was made to feel inadequate because her husband had an over-zealous appetite for other women; there are names attached to these victims. I know them personally. These victims were left holding the bag of shame, but they are not what they've been through. You are not what you've been through. Your past does not define you, but your bounce-back does. How you react to your adversity builds and determines your character.

My prayer for you is that as you confront your issues and face your giants, you will tap into that insurmountable strength and agility. No longer do you have to tiptoe in the tulips. You are not alone in your struggles. There are so many people in the grandstand of life rooting for your victory even when it doesn't seem like it. Go forth and face your challenges as God enables and instructs. Follow that still, small voice to your purpose, destiny, and victory. You are more courageous than you know. You are a conqueror. You are an overcomer. You are a giant slayer.

CHAPTER FOUR

Understanding Forgiveness

I spent approximately 15 years after the abuse ended trying to get a firm footing in life and suppressing memories. Over time, I decided to begin a journey to forgiveness and a quest to healing that freed me to really love myself first and then others. That revelation and evolution did not happen overnight, but everything else that I tried was a substitute for what I really needed. There was no quick resolution to my problems. I wish this book was a quick fix for you, but unfortunately it is not.

Forgiveness is a process that allows you to put an end to feelings of resentment and bitterness against someone who has offended you. The keyword in that sentence is process and that process is different for everyone. Even after you read this book, I am sure you will have more questions and more raw emotions that are directly attached to your pain. This process can be long and emotionally stressful, but it is worth it nonetheless. How quickly you can forgive is sometimes attached to the depth and magnitude of your pain. I could have easily forgiven my father for grounding me when I didn't think I deserved it, but the mental, sexual, and emotional anguish I suffered at his hands, took me years to resolve.

Forgiveness is healing. For most of the healing process, I didn't realize how emotionally and mentally scarred I was. I had learned to compensate by exuding my pain to others, but the pain was very present. It became an attachment or an extension of me that I carried around like a life-draining parasite. I cuddled my pain and the more I cuddled and fed into the offenses, the more magnified they became. The unforgiveness and pain had become so present until I forgot what life was like before the hurt. I became more aware of the inner workings of my heart through the Word of God and through love. I decided that I no longer wanted to pacify the hurt, but I wanted to be whole and emotionally healthy so that I could live a fulfilled life. Emotional healing had a cost and that cost was to forgive.

Forgiveness is powerful. My past situations no longer are allowed to continually have the power over my life. We are wired to protect ourselves and survive. Self-preservation is an important part of our first nature. It is natural for us to become defensive in the same manner in which our offense was delivered. To forgive we withhold our normal retaliatory actions and seek a better resolution. In other words, when we forgive, we undermine our first response coping mechanisms and exonerate our offender, whether we think they deserve it or not and whether they are repentant or not. Anyone who has been violated in such a manner can relate to how difficult that is. I can celebrate that God enabled me to fight for my sanity and my desire to thrive.

Most of those fights were tackled without the ability to voice the root of my pain because of the shame, embarrassment, and fear. The effects of any abuse can be extensive and deep and there were levels to my pain. As my life progressed and the different quirks surfaced, I forgave and forgave again. One big, blanketed "I forgive you" statement was not enough for me. There were times when I thought that I should be further along in life than I currently was. I forgave my father for making me stall and become stagnant. There were times when I wasn't as intimate with my husband as I could have been, so I forgave my father for making me cold and detached. There were times when I entertained the erroneous idea that all men were predatory. I, then forgave my father for making me prejudge. I still desired male companionship, but was too wounded to embrace or nurture it. At that point, I had to forgive my father for predisposing me to promiscuity. At different milestones and struggles in my life, God reminded me that I needed to deal with the links in the chain that still had me bound, intimidated, and embarrassed. The more I forgave him, the more empowered I became. Forgiveness empowered me to no longer be a victim. I am now able to celebrate the fact that I survived. I am a child abuse/incest survivor. My decision to forgive him doesn't lessen that fact.

Forgiveness does not make what happened to you any less real. I am not trying to minimize your pain or condone mistreatment. I am not asking you to sweep your issues under the rug and let bygones be bygones. You decide to disarm your emotions and to put yourself at the forefront of your pain when you forgive. This will not discredit or nullify your pain but it will put you in control of it.

Forgiveness is not apathy nor does it promote lawlessness. Just because you forgive does not mean that you should expose yourself to continual victimization. Protect yourself and if you must, seek legal help. Sometimes our offenders may have to face punitive charges if laws were broken. That does not mean that you didn't forgive them. There are consequences to actions. Forgiveness is not negated because a person seeks legal counsel when they are wronged. I struggled with that through my healing process. I believed that if I truly forgave my father I had to extend an olive branch to him to assure him that I had forgiven him. That is not true. I did not have to be passive to forgive. Forgiveness is work, but it is aggressive work. Work denotes labor. Forgiveness can be intense labor or an easy feat, but there are no shortcuts. I think one of the hardest facets of forgiveness is to forgive someone who has no remorse for the offenses they have committed against you. A simple apology can acknowledge the wrongdoing. When a person apologizes, it often validates the pain and their possible responsibility or role in causing it. When an offender does not own up to their responsibility, the victim is sometimes left with unanswered questions and in some cases, resentment.

The good news is you can forgive even if the offender never apologizes. No apology? That's no problem! There is no profit in remaining bitter and grudgeful, while waiting for another person to give you permission to move on with life. You move on regardless. Some people are unaware that you've even offended. They may never apologize. Why wait? By forgiving your offender, you expedite your healing process and you release the issue to God to solve. Hebrews 12:1 says, *"Wherefore seeing we also are compassed about with so great a cloud of witnesses, **let us lay aside every weight**, and the sin which doth so easily beset us, and let us run with patience the race that is set before us."* Lay aside the weight of unforgiveness even if your pain is never recognized by the offender. We should not expect the healing to come from the source that caused our pain. Allow the source within to spring up and catapult you into healing.

Revenge and retribution should not be a part of your healing process. The desire for revenge makes it difficult and almost impossible to forgive. Revenge or street justice is not a rational solution for the pain you have experienced. Sometimes revenge makes the situation worse by jump starting a vicious cycle where no one is healed. Getting even keeps you looking in the narrow rearview mirror of your life and takes your attention off the wide windshield that lies before you. Mahatma Gandhi said it best when he said, *"An eye for an eye only ends up making the whole world blind."* When you're preoccupied with revenge, your offender remains in a place of power in your life. Direct the energy that you've given to revenge towards something positive that takes the attention and focus away from your offender.

I understand that sometimes it is hard to shift attention and forgive especially if your pain is recent. Jesus forgave the people that crucified Him quickly. He made intercession for them as he took some of His last breaths. Although time does not heal, the element of time can make it easier to forgive. No one should set a timeframe on your pain. You should be allowed to experience your feelings of disappointment while actively pursuing healing and forgiveness. Psychologists have put the process of grief and loss in five stages: denial, anger, bargaining, depression, and acceptance. Pain and abuse victims find themselves going through those stages.

Denial is the stage of disbelief when the victim is in total shock and can hardly believe that the action is happening. Anger is the stage where reality is beginning to set in along with resentment. The hurting person exemplifies bargaining by pondering the "what ifs." At this stage, victims wonder if there was something that could have been done differently to avoid the situation altogether. The fourth stage is depression where intense sadness takes place. The last stage is acceptance. It is characterized by calmness and coping. These stages are not necessarily experienced by everyone and are not experienced in any specific order. Sometimes these stages are revisited and the victim finds themselves regressing to stages that they have already passed through.

It is unrealistic to expect healing and forgiveness if the victim is still being mistreated and abused. Some abusers assault and ask for forgiveness only to repeat the same cycle again as in the case of many domestic violence situations. This distorts trust and hinders the forgiveness process. During a storm of this caliber in your life, it is impossible to accurately assess the damages until the storm is over. Therefore, any forgiveness given now may indeed be premature and a form of pseudo-forgiveness. Also, an abuser that is in the repetitive cycle of assault then apologize, is not truly repentant. At that point, it is important to seek a safe haven since the abuser refuses to change. If you are compelled to abandon an abusive relationship, you can still forgive and heal. You do not have to remain in that situation to prove your forgiveness. Consider your safety first, then allow true forgiveness and healing to manifest while you are in a safe place.

Emotionally safe places are important to your overall recovery. Most safe places are centered around people that you have attracted on your road to healing. Be careful not to become overly dependent on people who wish to remain victims. These people can mean well, but inadvertently keep you on an emotional roller coaster. Hurting people attract other hurting people. Misery loves company. You should not connect with people just to throw one big finger-pointing pity party. This will hinder your forgiveness and emotional health. It is possible to gradually change friends or supportive relationships as you matriculate through the healing process. Always remain grateful to the people who encouraged you along the way, but remember you are not obligated to remain in relationships that are not fruitful or healthy. Your objective should be to move forward and have victory over toxic people and circumstances. Forgiveness is hard. Unforgiveness is harder. Choose life. Choose love.

FORGIVENESS

CHAPTER FIVE

The Case For Forgiveness

I was very fortunate to have both of my grandparents present in my life as I was growing up. Both served as matriarchs of their respective families after my grandfathers passed away. They were wise in a lot of ways and often spoke in clichés when they gave instructions. I can remember my maternal grandmother saying, "Don't burn your bridges." I thought she was saying not to burn your britches when I was younger. As an adult, I realized that she was trying to teach me the importance of keeping relationships intact if possible. This is especially true for family and those positive relationships that are assets and not liabilities. Conflicts can burn bridges. More so than conflicts, inadequate conflict resolution or the lack of resolution can burn bridges as well. I appreciate their instruction, but the logic behind what they taught was not always given. Some of the logic came to me as life progressed.

Another cliché that started surfacing was, "Let go and let God." This simply meant to surrender my grasp and allow God to rectify the situation. When I insisted on making my father pay for what he did, I had no peace. I wanted to witness his calamity and know that whatever punishment he received was a direct result of what he did to me. During those times, I had a flooding of negative emotions and pain in my heart. These bottled-up feelings, were comparable to spiritual Congestive Heart Failure (CHF). I am a registered nurse by profession so I often relate physical diagnoses to spiritual or emotional conditions. When I care for patients who are acutely ill with CHF they often suffer with weight gain, shortness of breath, and fatigue. That's exactly how it feels to carry around the weight of unforgiveness. If you are sluggish, weighted down from the heaviness of resentment, and having difficulty releasing or exhaling, it is time to take a deep breath and exhale. We should not have to carry burdens for years upon years. God made a way that we can exchange our cares for His peace.

A bombardment of emotions can also result in overwhelming stress, upset stomach, and even ulcers. Stressors are known to influence increase in blood pressure and blood glucose. These issues can increase your chances of heart attacks and strokes. Most times we don't know how stressed and emotionally drained we really are until we start to let things go and look back at our previous condition. The Center for Disease Control (CDC) reported in 2013 that heart disease was the leading cause of death for women in America. In this same report, the CDC recommended that women lower their stress levels and learn ways to effectively deal with stress. Living with bottled up anger and unforgiveness are not healthy coping skills. Proverbs 17:22 says, *"A merry heart doeth good like medicine; but a broken spirit drieth the bones."* Do your body a favor and increase the merriness in your heart.

As Isaiah prophesied the coming of the Messiah in the 61st chapter, he explains that he will exchange beauty for ashes, oil of joy for mourning, and a garment of praise for the spirit of heaviness. It is our job to give God the ashes, the mourning, and the spirit of heaviness. He will be sure to replace them with beauty, the oil of joy, and a garment of praise. Releasing is an act of our will. We release with a purpose to move forward. Psalms

55:22 says, "*Cast thy burden upon the Lord, and he shall sustain thee; he shall never suffer the righteous to be moved.*" Everything that matters to you, matters to God. First Peter 5:7 says, "*Casting all your care upon him; for he careth for you.*" The metamorphosis from victim to victor did not take place until I released my urge to handle it and my desire for revenge.

I realized that it is not my job to make sure that I am avenged, if at all. Before I got to this point, most of the people that I had a relationship with had unknowingly felt my pain in some way. As long as I remained a victim in my mind, I was bound to hurt somebody. I subconsciously carried hurt from one relationship to the next, waiting and wanting someone to apply salve to my wounds. When this did not happen, I attempted to hurt them like I was hurting. No one really had the ability to reach the depths of my pain. I was reckless, hard and went overboard to show men that they had no power over me. I had been overpowered before and there was no way I was allowing that to happen again.

I needed healing from the inside out because my pain had become a cycle that I pulled other people into. This was my coping mechanism. It was undeniably wrong, but I felt justified in what I was doing. Hurting people will hurt other people but no one deserves to pay for crimes that they did not commit. That is what I did repeatedly. I charged people with another person's crimes. That behavior did not automatically stop on the day I walked up to my father and said, "I forgive you." I had to purpose in my heart not to allow another person to pay for his indiscretions. That is how you take control and start to regain your power.

Regaining your power, is another reason why we forgive. The powerlessness that I felt during the time that I was abused was astounding. I had no voice because I had been muted and sworn into secrecy. The powerlessness turned into intimidation and fear to the point of just to hear my father's footsteps would literally make me feel as if my heart was escaping my chest. The feeling returned for a second as I wrote those words. When we experience this level of powerlessness, we are subject to whatever happens so our desire is to take control any way we can. So, I entertained the thought of suicide once or twice and formulated a plan to do so at least once. The reasons for this were because 1) my innocence had been stolen, 2) my virtue had been squandered, 3) my nakedness had been uncovered, and 4) my power had been taken. My only recourse was knowing that I was smart. My ability to make excellent grades was the empowerment that I had at that time. Aside from school, I felt ugly, dirty, misused, unappreciated, unfit, and the list goes on.

As we forgive, our positive self-image starts to return. We repossess the power that was illegally taken. Our authoritative voice becomes restored and no longer do we have to remain victims and allow ourselves to be stripped again. We need our voices to encourage ourselves. One of the best weapons we have is the authority of our own words spoken to ourselves. If you are angry, unforgiving, and powerless, what do you say to yourself? Your voice changes how you see yourself and how you proceed to your destiny. At some of my lowest points, I had to talk to me, not in a psychotic way, but in an affirming way. I remember feeling like I was lost and misplaced. I said, "Girl, you are too good for this. You are smarter than this. Get up." I became stronger with every statement of affirmation. The more I forgave and affirmed myself, the more empowered I became to tell my story.

You forgive so that your empowerment will become someone else's empowerment. To open your mouth and tell your story can be scary. After all, who really wants to hear this? What will they think of me? The very first time I told my story, I was scolded. I was not supposed to say such things, but remain a lady and keep them hidden. The old saying, "What goes on in your house, stays in your house," was very much alive. I did not tell the story for years after it wasn't received well the first time. Now that I feel safe and more equipped to share, I do.

I am freer now than I have ever been. I released control of the story through the power of forgiveness. No longer do I have to keep the story in a controlled environment. As a matter of fact, this book is a result of me releasing how far the story reaches, but at the same time controlling my healing through the power of Jesus Christ. The more I shared the story the more empowered I became. My truth is my truth. I no longer center my attention on the person who did it or why it was done because I have chosen to tell my story from the vantage point of forgiveness and victory. My story is my choice to divulge. I have totally and unconditionally forgiven.

For a long time, I thought and was told that I was to blame for the sexual abuse. My mindset would have never changed if I never started to forgive and share my life. Don't allow yourself to be shamed out of your testimony. Your testimony is your power to overcome. The first part of Revelation 12:11 says, *"And they overcame him by the blood of the Lamb, and the word of their testimony."* Memories still come, but I continue to

41

thank God that through Him, I can live a life unashamed, unafraid and empowered. More importantly than all of this, I wanted to make sure the integrity of God's forgiveness in my life remained intact.

I forgive because I am forgiven. I forgive because I want nothing to change the fact that I will also need God's forgiveness extended to me. My treatment of others on my road to recovery was not justified just because I had been abused. Those people were collateral damage. I can't expect God's forgiveness if I didn't forgive my father. In Matthew 18, Peter began to question Jesus about forgiveness. Jesus answered Peter in a parable which is sometimes called The Parable of the Unforgiving Servant. In the parable, there is a servant who needed to settle his debts with a king; however, the servant did not have the money that was owed. The king wanted to assume custody of the servant's wife and children until the servant could settle his debt.

The servant was distraught and pleaded with the king to not take his family. The king had mercy on the servant and erased all his debts. The same servant was owed a much smaller debt by one of his own peers, a fellow servant. The peer did not have the money to settle with the servant. The unforgiving servant was not merciful or forgiving to his peer. When the king heard this, he reminded the unforgiving servant of his previous situation where he was shown mercy. The king refused to remain merciful to the unforgiving servant and had him thrown in prison. This must be what we look like when we decide to hold grudges and be resentful with another person. Since my King, Jesus, gave me a clean slate of forgiveness, I am not concerned about how, when, or if my father ever must pay his debts. My debts have been settled.

To double-down on the reciprocity of forgiveness, Galatians 6:7 says, *"Be not deceived; God is not mocked; for whatsoever a man soweth, that shall he also reap."* I have not always been this conscientious about the way I handle conflicts and challenges as I am now. I want to sow and reap grace and mercy. I want to sow and reap forgiveness. In the Lord's Prayer, we are instructed to pray that as we forgive others, we also receive forgiveness. Jesus set that precedence of prayer in his example to his disciples. In Mark 11:24-26, Jesus spoke to the disciples about praying and forgiveness. He tells them that when they pray, they need to forgive. In that passage, it seems that the answers to our prayers are also predicated upon our ability to forgive others. He concludes in verse 26 by saying if we don't forgive, we will not be forgiven. This does not mean we must do extra stuff to prove that we have forgiven or place ourselves in harm's way. It simply means we need to make sure that we forgive others. We don't have the right to choose what we are willing to forgive. We can't excuse the little white lie and not the others. We forgive all because forgiveness is not restricted to certain offenses and it is perpetual. We need forgiveness more often than we know. We should extend the same forgiveness to others that we are expecting to receive. Our objective should be to take the high road in every situation if possible.

CHAPTER SIX

Forgiving by Faith, Through Love

If I didn't have the capacity and will to forgive, the title of this book would be very different. The spirit in which it was written would be different. God strengthened and graced me to matriculate through the process of forgiveness without residual hate. The process I used may differ from another survivor's in some areas, but the steps below are those that worked for me.

1.   **I confronted my feelings.** The first chapter was about confronting the past. This is different. The first chapter expounded upon confronting the event or memory of the event that caused the emotions. This step refers to confronting the emotions. Feelings can improve, but not by ignoring them. I had to face my feelings head on. That meant, that I could no longer avoid talk

shows and other shows that dealt with the deep issues of abuse, no longer would I blame myself, and I could cry if I wanted to.

2.   **Counteracted my feelings with scriptural defense.** For example, if I was feeling fearful, powerless, hateful, or as if I would lose my mind, I would meditate on 2 Timothy 1:7, *"For God has not given us a spirit of fear, but of power, and of love, and of a sound mind."* If I felt pain I would read how God collected my tears in a bottle in Psalms 56:8 and how He would exchange my ashes of mourning for beauty in Isaiah 61:3. The Word became my Counselor.

3.   **Identify the real enemy.** Even though people perform the acts, Satan has been the enemy from the beginning. His objective was to steal, kill, and destroy me (John 10:10). Our main enemy is not people, but spiritual wickedness in high places (Ephesians 6:12). This may seem as if I deflected the blame. I know we have a choice in how we respond to temptations. I did not identify my real opponent so that I could shift the blame, but I needed to understand better who I was up against.

4.   **Refused to avoid my offender.** I had been bound enough. I was not about to over-compromise to avoid him.

5.   **Removed the need to get even**. I wanted to kill him at times. I had imagined ways to make him suffer. After all, I had been violated. Eventually those feelings of retribution subsided. I no longer needed to avenge myself.

6.   **Released my offender from the need to "make it up" to me**. I felt that I was owed. There was something due to me that I really had no clue of. No amount of money or gifts could pay me for my sufferings. He really did not have the capacity to compensate me for my pain. Even without an apology, I released him. I will talk more about lack of apologies later in the book.

7.   **Through all of the above six steps, I prayed**. My execution of the six steps was not perfect. I stumbled. I fell. I recollected myself and the cycle happened again and again. Eventually, I stumbled less and my falls became near misses and I began to regain my bearings easier and quicker.

FORGIVENESS

It is difficult to say that God's grace was anywhere in this gruesome story. I beg to differ. There were many opportunities for my story to end negatively. Nevertheless, most of the results have been favorable for me. I can remember feeling so helpless until I attempted to hang myself on a plant hook that was in the ceiling of our home. That wasn't the only time that I felt suicidal, but that was the only time that I created a plan. Just the fact that I am alive today is enough for me to appreciate the favor of God. Favor then increased my faith.

My faith journey began when I was 23 years old. I stood before a church in a traditional altar call proclaiming my desire to escape my old life. It remains a mystery to me of how I made it to that altar that Sunday morning. I'm sure that I still had the high and stench of alcohol and marijuana from the previous night. I had also gotten up that morning from the bed with a man that was not my husband. I went to that altar though and I looked into that pastor's eyes and proclaimed my desire for salvation. All the old habits that I had did not just fall away, but my confession changed the trajectory for my life. Over the next five years following that, my life changed. The caterpillar was turning into a butterfly. I had faith to believe that a life in Christ could heal my broken areas and change me from the inside out. Not only did my faith change me, but it gave me the ability to forgive.

Faith enables us to forgive whether our struggle is with others or ourselves. Faith will bring us to defining moments in our lives that will force us to choose to believe God or the circumstances. My circumstances were ugly, but I was assured in God. That is faith, a blessed assurance. Faith became active in me. Therefore, I actively pursued forgiveness by faith. Through that same lens, I could see my father actively pursuing my forgiveness, but without words. Those two faith efforts together brought me to full forgiveness. Faith supplemented when an apology was not extended.

In Galatians 5:6, we learn that faith works through love. I forgave through faith because of my love. You can forgive through faith and love as well. This is the ministry of Jesus to be intentional and strategic in our extension of love and restoration. John 3:17 explains that Jesus did not come to condemn us, but to offer salvation to us through Him. His mission was intentional and deliberate. The mission eventually led him through a very human moment in Gethsemane to become a curse on a cross at Calvary. What a sacrifice! The revelation of His love for me motivated me to forgive for the simple offenses as well as the heinous, but to overcome this, the faith and love had to become intentional as well. We cannot depend upon the element of time.

Forgiveness does not just happen over time. There is an old cliché' that says, "Time heals all wounds." That is not necessarily true. There was a woman in the Bible being afflicted by the same issue of blood for twelve years. (Luke 8:43-48) Time did not heal her. She heard of a healer coming to town. She got out of her house and made her way to Him. Her strategy was, "If I could but touch." She became intentional about her health and as a result, she received a healing touch from Jesus that got His attention and made her whole. Intention is a component that we must add to the element of time. We must be as intentional as we are when we place one foot in front of the other to walk. **The first step in being intentional is to decide to move forward.**

Make a verbal declaration to yourself that you will move from a position of pain to one of healing, from bitterness to joy, then add corresponding actions to your declaration. I can still remember my verbal declaration. I said, "Devil you had my childhood, but you will not have my adulthood." I have grown quite a bit since then and I realize that he really did not have my childhood. However, the declaration worked for me back then. **Next, define why this deliberate move is important to you and the**

ones you love. Purpose will encourage you to set realistic goals. My desire was to clear my mind enough so that I could function in this world. I wanted to be a good mother to my children, be a good wife to my husband, and live free of feeling inadequate and incomplete. I can remember watching *Rudolph the Red-nosed Reindeer* cartoon during the Christmas season. Some of the broken and rejected toys were taken to the Island of the Misfit Toys. In my mind, that is where I was, but I was refusing to stay. My purpose was to escape. **Lastly,**

remain focused. Memories of sexual trauma evaded my mind space so many times. I took a step forward, then felt unworthy, and took two steps backwards. Over time, I started comparing my life progression with the progress of successful family members and classmates because I was either stagnant or staggering towards a lucrative career. I knew I had to be productive because I was the oldest child of my family and I had children of my own. I had a deep desire to be an example for my siblings and my children. I had to shift my focus back to my purpose. Thank God I defeated the memories, but that does not mean that I still don't have them.

Dark memories and horrifying flashbacks still come. Sometimes they come at the most inopportune time. I have had them during times of intimacy with my husband, when my children sat on male relatives' laps, or when a male stood too closely to me in the grocery store line. I hated that I saw almost every male as a potential predator. Forgiving almost came easier than forgetting, but since I oversee my recovery, I became committed to both.

You can as well. I know the forgiving and forgetting seems impossible. You won't forget in the literal sense of the word. You don't have selective amnesia nor should you desire to suppress difficult memories; however, you can choose what you meditate on. Traumatic memories don't own me nor do they own you. I own them. I control how I process them. You control how you process your difficult past. I released every vision of revenge and every expectation of recompense. I am emancipated because I forgot. I do not expect an apology. I forgot his debt to me. I forgave his debt to me. I desired an apology to validate my pain years ago, now I don't have that deep desire anymore. Although I would love to hear him take responsibility for his action, my father doesn't owe me a thing. I had to let that go to move on. I had expectations of a fairy tale apology, but since that never happened, I released my expectations. The constant expecting kept me angry, disappointed and frustrated by my ability to love.

Even as I write this book, my aim is not to humiliate him. Later in this book, I will talk about the very powerful conversation my father and I had during this book writing process. In writing this transparent account of things that transpired during some very dark moments, my goal is to teach forgiveness from the authority of a person who has had to forgive. So, while I have forgotten in one sense, I am very lucid in another. I can't be so forgetful of my past until I refuse to use my testimony to help someone else. I paid for this story in my body, in my mind, and in my spirit and in doing so I paid for the freedom to share it. So, I share my very personal story, my personal truth with you for my deliverance and for the deliverance of other people that have experienced the atrocities of abuse.

FORGIVENESS

CHAPTER SEVEN

Unlimited and Unconditional

Forgiveness isn't only about letting go, but it includes healing and restoration. For this reason, we should desire to keep our hearts free of discord and offense. In other words, forgiveness should become our way of life. Our ability to forgive should be unlimited and unconditional to everyone. "Matthew 18:21, Peter asks Jesus about forgiveness. He attempted to pin Jesus to an exact number of how many times to forgive a person who might sin against him. Peter thought the number should be seven times a day. I am almost certain that Peter was shocked when Jesus replied in verse 22, "seventy times seven." In this passage, Jesus is not giving us permission to stop being merciful. He is not expecting us to keep a running count and then cut off forgiveness at the 490th offense. He was explaining to us to be perpetual in forgiveness. We forgive daily and perpetual as the love of God undergirds or empowers us to do so. We are empowered to forgive because of the love and forgiveness that God gives to us. For that reason, every opportunity to forgive should be laced with love, a love for others and a love for self. Love then answers the question of how we forgive and why we forgive. We forgive through love and we forgive because of love. I loved my father before the abuse started and I still appropriately love him today. While I was trapped in the matrix of abuse, I wasn't so sure about loving anyone especially the person who had warped my idea of love. At times, I wanted to wish death on him, but I was too afraid that what I wished on him might become my fate. Over time and through the love and Word of God, my capacity to extend agape love has returned. Love forgives. Loves does not wish ill will. Love does not seek revenge. Love is the catalyst, the motivation, and the fuel for every selfless act that we do.

In John 3:16, we find that the fundamental reason God sent Jesus to the earth was His love for mankind. When we read through the New Testament we see that Jesus was moved with compassion prior to most of his miracles. Love is the reason Jesus withstood the public humiliation, the beating at the scourging post, and the crucifixion on the cross. In my opinion, His love for mankind had more power to hold Jesus to the cross than the nails had.

Jesus' obedience to the cross raised the bar of forgiveness for us. This new grace made forgiveness and salvation available to everyone and mostly everything. We should be an extension of that forgiveness as we forgive unconditionally. Your ability to forgive cannot be limited to someone's failure to repay ten dollars that they borrowed from you. Our forgiveness must be able to cover even the things that seem as taboo as incest, rape, child molestation, and the things as heinous as the murder of children, senior citizens, or anyone for that matter. Our community is currently grappling with the abduction and murder of a six-year-old child as I write this book. Suspects have been arrested, but of course by our statutes they are innocent until proven guilty. As awful and tragic as this crime is, there is forgiveness available for the culprits.

Murder of an innocent child is heart-wrenching and difficult to forgive. Sexual abuse and exposing someone to a forced abortion is difficult to forgive. However, God did not restrict our mandate to forgive to only certain offenses. He knew horrible circumstances would arise. He also knew that we could endure, survive, and overcome. We may have staggered because of the punches that we received, but we did not give up. Your stagger may be longer than expected, but as soon as you get your bearings, quickly forgive. Jesus addressed His issues immediately and that should be our goal as well.

Quick forgiveness, slow arousal to anger, tenderheartedness and patience are God's standards. The principle of "an eye for an eye" has been replaced with love and grace. Holding a grudge does not require great strength, but releasing one does. Jesus was simply amazing in that while he took his last breaths, he made sure that He interceded for the forgiveness of the people who put Him on the cross. He uttered to the Father, *Forgive them; for they know not what they do,* in Luke 23:34. He went so far as to forgive a thief that was on the neighboring cross. The quicker we decide to forgive our offender, the quicker we are able to move on to healing and restoration.

Forgiveness is not limited to other people, sometimes you must forgive yourself. I wrestled with self-condemnation after being fed lies that I caused or wanted an incestuous relationship with my father. This is common for sexual abuse survivors and people who think they failed in relationships. It is also common for the abusers to attempt to fault the victim. When victims feel that they are at fault, they are less likely to tell. The guilt is silencing. Even when I would give private testimonies about the abuse, I left out parts. I refused to talk about the abortion much because of the shame. I thought surely God would require my life for the life of the unborn child. The thoughts plagued me so much until I had visions of what the child might have looked like. As I got older, I would downplay my thoughts by imagining the child with birth defects because of the incestuous conception. No longer do I have to overthink or downplay it. I released all of that responsibility because it was never mine to own. I am exonerated from the guilt of the abuse and the abortion. I didn't have a choice so that is someone else's guilt to pick up and work through if they so desire.

There is one more heart-wrenching issue that I had to deal with, that I had to forgive and release myself from. That issue was the death of my child's father. He was a young and healthy 24-year-old man who was basically a homebody whenever we were living together on good terms. However, whenever I would ask him to leave, he would hang out with friends more. When the car accident occurred, he was out with friends. I picked up the guilt at that time because I felt that if I had allowed him to be home, he would not have been out that night. The truth of the matter is I most likely picked up that guilt because I couldn't control the outcome and therefore, had difficulties dealing with the pain.

FORGIVENESS

Realistically speaking, some things are beyond our control. That's life. We can pray for favorable outcomes, but sometimes the outcomes are different from what we prayed for. If I had the ability to stop that car wreck that night, I would have stopped it. If I had the ability to make him walk out of that hospital, I would have done whatever was necessary to make that happen. I came to the realization that his destiny was not in my hands. Since I could not control that outcome, I decided to let that guilt go.

Sometimes the fact that we can't control all our outcomes, makes us blame God because He is omniscient. We know that He is a good God so we have problems understanding hardships. It is true that He is all-powerful, but He is not a dictator. He is not a big hand in the sky that moves people around like pawns on a chessboard. I wish he could have moved me around a few times and insisted that I be obedient. I would be so much farther ahead right now. He gives us the choice to adhere to His Word or to listen to that small, still voice or not. Bottom line is, there is a human element involved in this life and in our destiny. We do not get the opportunity to live in a utopia, free of any tribulations simply because we are Christians. God remains sovereign. He is able with our permission and our surrendering to help us draw something beautiful out of the things we know to be gaping and horrific.

CHAPTER EIGHT

Give Wounds Oxygen

Both physical and emotional wounds need oxygen to heal. Some things need to be uncovered to allow nature to take its course. The cover-up can smother, but it cannot heal. Smothering pain still smolders and the moment the cover is lifted, the stench and burn of the pain resurfaces. We expose our wounds so that we can begin to have new, healthy relationships or to rebuild some of the old ones that have disintegrated.

God is relational and created us to be relational as well. From the very beginning, we see Him saying that it is not good that man should be alone in Genesis 2:18. We are all interconnected in the grand scheme of things. We form kindred relationships, romantic relationships, and friendships where we become comfortable and vulnerable. Distant or non-familial relationships have the least ability to sting. Most of the time when we are in intimate relationships and communities, disappointments happen. Depending on the severity, these disappointments can possibly put relationships at a standstill in a proverbial "fork in the road." In this chapter, we will discuss moving past the pain and forgiveness.

It is no surprise that most of the time our greatest pain comes through the people we love or the people we hold in high regard. No relationship is free from the strain of disagreements, even our Christian relationships. For most of us, our church can become a makeshift family. We eat, worship, and raise our children together, and learn together. By no means are church members or church leaders perfect. We expect more from our church family because we expect them to operate on a higher level of integrity. Even in that, disappointments happen.

How do we move forward in a strained church relationship? I have never experienced "church hurt," but as I stated before, my father became a pastor while the sexual abuse was still occurring. I did not, even at my young age, allow my father's conduct to determine who God was to me. I did not judge God's integrity by the integrity that man displayed even though he was supposed to be a representative of Christ. I did not turn away from Christ because of what I experienced. My childhood experiences catapulted me to an even more intimate relationship with Christ because I realized that only He could ease into the innermost parts of my being to heal and recover.

In these times of conflict, you should be even more dependent on your relationship in Christ. Divide and conquer had been an evil tactic since creation. We allow minor disagreements and misunderstandings to divide us on a large scale. You cannot tuck tail and run from every relationship just because of minor disagreements. That was my survival tactic. To avoid being hurt, I would abandon relationships for the most minute reasons. In these latter years, God is making me stay the course. That does not mean that those relationships will be intact until death, but at least you can run the course of the relationship. And most of the time, you will know that that era of your life is ending.

Pain in family relationships can be both different and difficult because we expect the course of those relationships to last forever. Our paths are so intertwined that we can't see life apart from them. However, because our relationships within our families are so familiar we forget to give proper attention to hardcore issues. We brush off issues that should be dealt with collectively whether it's by family meetings, prayers, counseling, or simple apologies. I have seen the conflict resolution strategy in families range from loud and ineffective yelling to sweeping the issues under the rug and ignoring the fact that they even occurred. It is easy to ignore a person cutting us off in traffic and making obscene gestures except for a few cases of road rage, but when we ignore family issues most likely they will resurface. They resurface because we still have access to each other. They resurface because we didn't effectively deal with them. Issues don't die down. They should be nipped in the bud so that they do not become generational curses passed on from one era to the next. That is the story of King David. He was a man after God's own heart, but he attempted to cover or ignore several issues within his family. For that reason, his family experienced deceit, murder, rape, and treason. The seeds of several of his sons were cut off because they experienced premature death. Family was important then and it still is today.

Families are the very woven fabric of our society and to see those relationships disintegrate is disheartening. I could have been justified in severing ties with my father if that is what I desired. That was not what my heart led me to do. For many of the years after the abuse, I was drilled on my duty to keep him in a place of honor so that grew in me. However, what was brewing under the surface was the desire to be free. I realize that the relationship between me and my father is not the same. I basically can't remember exactly how the relationship was because the "nervous breakdown" happened when I was seven. However, I do remember being a tomboy and wanting to learn everything he knew about outdoors stuff. I can remember him teaching me how to fish, do vehicle maintenance, chop wood for the fireplace, mow the yard, and learn a few carpentry techniques. Those were the bright spots in our relationship. Even during the abuse, some of those patches of normalcy remained during daytime hours. I clung to those spots because they were the times when I felt like a daughter. Eventually the abuse took over and those bright spots were no longer welcomed by me. The flame diminished and I became distant and cold for the most part.

We don't share father-daughter embraces, but we do an occasional fist bump or a one-arm hug. Boundaries are hard in family relationships because there are other members who are also affected. I added a realistic view and boundaries to my forgiveness to salvage and reinvent the relationship we have. Realistically, we can't act like nothing happened nor can we travel back in time and recoup a stellar relationship;

but I have come to grips with how far I am willing to go in the current relationship. For example, I have not been able to say, "Happy Father's Day," but I can write it or buy a gift. It is doable for me. My boundaries and realistic approach might not work for everyone. Your boundaries must be individualized to meet your needs, views, values, and desires.

Each case is different. I heard a wise woman say that after a bomb goes off in a relationship, wait until the debris, ashes, and soot settle and then assess your damages. In other words, you must evaluate your relationship including past and present behaviors. If all parties involved are willing to sincerely repair the relationship and move forward, sometimes it is worth giving it another try. This is especially true and very important in resolving conflicts in marriages. I have been married for sixteen years to my wonderful husband, Anderson. God has been good to us, but we have had issues to arise in our marriage as most marriages do. There is no such thing as a perfect marriage. In marriage, there are two different people from two different backgrounds with many different values and belief systems merging into one union. This will not happen by simply saying "I do." There will be misunderstandings. One rule of thumb is to pursue the principle in Ephesians 4:26, "Be ye angry, and sin not. Let not the sun go down on your anger." We have not always done it perfectly, but we try not to allow feelings of offense to linger and fester. Often our first responses following the misunderstanding will determine how we resolve our issues.

As Anderson and I began our life together, we began to experienced what I call, "merging pains". "Merging Pains" are those pains and strains that marriages can experience as the two individuals become one. By the fifth year of our marriage, I was entertaining the idea of divorce. This was most likely attributed to my attempt to run away again. One day I called one of my friends to tell her that I wanted a divorce. She was the objective voice I needed. She did not co-sign on my suggestions, but instead listened and challenged my thoughts. She was a very much needed sounding board. Afterwards, I prayed about it and did not feel a release in my heart. It seemed as though I could hear God saying, "NO." That was eleven years ago, I have not entertained that thought again. God has matured us both as individuals and as a couple. We now realized that forgiveness was a key player in our marriage. When we forgive each other, we let it go. We don't rehash things that we have forgiven.

The institution of marriage is also a pillar in our society. Marriage has been a part of the American Dream for decades now. People desire careers, homes, spouses, children, and a white picket fence. Marriage is more than a coveted experience, but marriage is a covenant relationship that has been under attack since Eden. Don't be so quick to throw in the towel. Sometimes we put more time, commitment, and detail into weddings than we do the actual marriages. We can't be apt to drop the gavel on our spouses at the sign of the first mistake. My life was never in danger in my marriage. We never had an abusive relationship so I didn't have to run for safety when I was disappointed. I do empathize and understand when people must do that, but I could stand still and seek God to repair the broken areas.

One of the things I had to do as God repaired my marriage was to quiet the crowd. You should be meticulous about who you are receiving advice from for your marriage. I never sought advice from family, even the family members with successful marriages. Sometimes people can see your faults and forget about the struggles they had as their marriages grew. Even without soliciting for advice, I heard *insane wisdom*. Insane wisdom is outrageous and unconventional nuggets of knowledge that have no sensible foundation or backing. Sometime people who use insane wisdom to try to prove their point by using biblical scriptures out of context or old wives' tales. Please don't fall for the insane wisdom. I was once told to keep a spare tire, meaning a man on the side, just in case my husband failed. They used a scripture to justify this practice saying that the Bible says, "Don't let your right hand know what your left hand is doing." If you desire healing and restoration in your marriage, being deceitful and unfaithful will not help. Give your whole heart to the restoration process.

FORGIVENESS

CHAPTER NINE

Rediscover Yourself

You suffered punches and attacks that could have taken you out. The overcomer in you escaped. You survived for a reason. I survived for a reason. We survived extrinsic and self-inflicted wounds. For nearly a full twelve months after my child's father passed, I spiraled down a slope that could have easily led to my death. I changed friends and addresses. My weight dropped without any effort from me. I self-medicated with marijuana and alcohol. There was a never-ending party when I was around people. When the people were gone, I realized just how lonely and mentally perplexed I was. I wanted to self-destruct because I felt that it was unfair for me to live and be happy after my child's father left this earth so early. I can clearly see now that it was the love I had for my daughters that kept me from experimenting with other drugs. That love pulled me back from an abyss that was plagued by drugs, alcohol, parties, and promiscuity.

The love for them sustained me until I learned to love and embrace myself. Eventually, I started giving myself permission to be happy and experience joy again. I rediscovered me by embracing myself and my identity in Christ.

Rediscovery is a crucial stage in the healing process. Rediscovery means to find something again that was lost or forgotten. We can be so cognizant and engulfed by what someone did to us that we lose sight of our identity. During rediscovery, you should try to learn more about you. You are a different person than you were when you were scorned. You are now the person who is forgiving and seeking healing. So, you may find out new and interesting details about you as you discover what is fulfilling for you.

The first part of the rediscovery process is to **reimagine your life**. You have experienced what pain is. Now, you should imagine what healing and happiness are. If you can't picture it, you probably can't produce it. See yourself emotionally healthy, having the fulfillment you desire. Imagine yourself laughing, dancing, and enjoying enriching relationships. Paint a clear picture of what happiness looks like to you. This includes writing a precise plan that maps out a way to accomplish your desires. As I re-imagined my life, I journaled very often. As I revisited my journal entries, I was able to add faith to what I had written to bring about a positive change.

I am amazed at how close I have gotten to what I imagined when I go back to read my journal. Journaling was a very instrumental outlet that allowed me to write my dreams, imaginations, and hopes during the rediscovery stage.

During rediscovery, you also can **redefine who you are**. We are different in the different seasons of our lives. I defined myself by several unplanned pregnancies, alcohol, drugs, and partying in a very broken season. Even after the wildness was over, I defined myself by what I thought people expected of me. We can't allow the perceptions and ideas of people and society to encapsulate us. I began to establish an authentic identity after the wildness and my many attempts to conform to society's standards were over. As the metamorphosis started to take place in my life, no longer did I have to crawl. The crawling limited my view and slowed me down. I eventually allowed the transformation from a caterpillar to butterfly to take place. My short caterpillar legs were no longer needed because I had gotten my wings. Define who you are in this season despite how you were in the past.

On a sheet of paper I want you to print the word "Victim" in the center and draw a small circle around it. I want you to write everything you can think of that brought you pain and disappointment. On a separate sheet of paper, I want you to write your name and the words, "the survivor." Then draw a circle around those words. Write everything that you can think of about your victorious life around those words. Tuck the "Victim" paper away so that you can revisit it later and see your growth. Put your "Survivor" paper in a clear document protector. Place that paper somewhere where you can see it everyday. As you read the words of survival, you will gain more strength to move forward and to redefine who you are. You have that power and opportunity to write the ending to your own story.

Lastly, you **rebuild yourself** by considering your worth, value, and needs. When a person's spirit has been broken or crushed, it is important to add rebuilding to the recovery process. Your greatest influence and affirmations should come from you and your belief systems. Your worth should not be determined by someone else's perception, but we must actively work on how you esteem yourself. I rebuild myself with affirming scriptures. I say about myself what God says. Please see the Appendix, for affirming scriptures that you can say to build yourself up.

After every disappointment, we should pick ourselves up, dust ourselves off, and give life another shot. We are much stronger than we know, but in the rediscovery process, you must learn what activates your strength. One of the key things for me was laughter. Proverbs 17:22 says, "A *merry heart does good like medicine.*" Laughter can become like medicine to your body. The latter part of verse 22 says that a crushed spirit dries up the bones. Reject the temptation to be dry. I have laughed when I didn't necessarily feel like it, but that was the antidote to my despair. Medicine doesn't always taste or feel good, but we are willing to try it because the doctor ordered it. Our Great Physician has ordered laughter for our emotional well-being and we have a promise from Him that laughter yields good results.

In other times, I developed or revisited old hobbies that I had allowed to go to the wayside. Hobbies are rewarding and help to relieve stress. I enjoyed reading, fishing, writing, and crossword puzzles during my downtime. Hobbies add depth to who you are as a person by increasing the layers to your identity. Hobbies also give you more to do in your downtime instead of allowing yourself to be idle and passive. Hobbies are also conversation pieces that can help to establish new friendships. Put your hands to doing something that you enjoy. Reading, writing, and crossword puzzles are hobbies that I do in my private time. Fishing is a hobby that I could do with friends. Find your personal hobby and one that you could enjoy with other people.

FORGIVENESS

In quieter times, meditation was vital for me to rediscover who I was. My meditation consisted of having moments alone with God by making myself available in a quiet space with a scripture in my heart. Meditation isn't a time to sit around and think about heartaches, but it is a time to appreciate and celebrate victories. Meditation helps us to be aware of ourselves and the presence of God. Other benefits of meditation includes helping us to concentrate and to be focused, (Psalm 119:15); helping our understanding, (Psalm 119:27); inclining our hearts to worship ,(Psalm 1:2); and helping us to understand how to apply what we learn, (Joshua 1:8). Meditation also helps to invoke the peace of God. In Isaiah 26:3, we learn that the Lord will keep us in perfect peace if our mind is stayed on Him. We keep our mind in peace by thinking and meditating on things that are of a good report (Philippians 4:8).

You want to be a whole person in the next phase of your life. These concepts of the rediscovery stage are vital to your healing, recovery, and ultimately your future. This is your opportunity to establish the importance of your well-being for a change. You are definitely worth it.

CHAPTER TEN

Restarting Relationships

Be diligent and patient in the rediscovery phase. You will appreciate it once you begin to form new relationships. Your worth is not measured by your ability to be in a relationship, no matter the type. Sometimes we are so eager to have companionships that we forget to stop and smell the roses. Smell the fragrance of this moment while understanding that if you mishandle the rose there is always a chance of getting pricked by thorns.

As stated earlier, I went through a previous divorce. I think we were two people who had good intentions, but for some reason, we could not master the art of togetherness. Before the ink dried on the divorce papers and before we could even agree to the terms, I had already begun a new relationship. I gave myself no time and space to heal in between. Sometimes we use new relationships to heal us of the pain from the last. That is unfair to people, but it also unfair to yourself.

FORGIVENESS

If you truly want to be fulfilled in friendships and other intimate relationships, make a decision to not live in the same rotten place you have before. The Word of God says in Mark 2:22, that no one should put new wine into an old flask. The newness of the wine would disintegrate the flask and the wine will then be spilt. This principle can be used in the formation of new relationships as well. You shouldn't start a new relationship under the same stressful conditions. Each relationship has enough challenges of its own without dragging in old disappointments, prejudgments, and hurts. Start fresh and anew, with appropriate vigilance, but without judgements predicated upon your past.

Vigilance means to be careful, but not fearful and anxious. Fear and anxiety can cause you to not venture out and form new relationships. You were not created to be a lonely couch potato. We should intentionally be brave. Past relationship failures should not consume your ability to start over. Contrary to popular belief, bad things do happen to good people, but you do not have to lie down and succumb to your injuries. Get up, tighten your bootstraps, square your shoulders, and march forward as soon as you can. Trust yourself, your intuitions, and the Holy Spirit enough to warn you of impending dangers. Don't allow desperation to silence your red flags. You deserve someone who is comfortable with the rehabilitated, renewed, and restored YOU. Don't settle for anything less than that. This advice holds true whether you are ready for a new friendship or new courtship. Along with trusting yourself and trusting God, you must learn to trust others.

Trusting is hard because there is a level of vulnerability associated with it. If you've had a series of disappointments, you may be reluctant to trust; however, there is no real relationship of substance aside from trust. There are levels to the trust you extend. We shouldn't start a brand new relationship, allowing a stranger access to your home, children, bank account, and intimacy. That is blind and unwise trust. No one should go "all-in" into a new relationship. Premature full trust is certain to make you shed unnecessary tears in the future. Trust your gut feelings instead of emotions and desperations. Any new relationship can be exciting, but set a comfortable pace with realistic boundaries. Don't be rushed or pressured into commitments that you are uncomfortable with. We are on a quest for healing and not repetitive sorrows.

Allow yourself to be fulfilled in a relationship. No one human can satisfy every need that you have, but at least open your heart. Don't apply too much pressure on people to satisfy all the longings of your innermost being. They can't measure up to that mandate because people are flawed themselves. I was taught that only Jesus can reach that deeply into us. Jesus said in Luke 4:18, *"The Spirit of the Lord is upon me, because he hath anointed me to preach the gospel to the poor; he hath sent me to heal the brokenhearted, to preach deliverance to the captives, and recovering of sight to blind, to set at liberty them that are bruised."* Healing and deliverance is available for the broken-hearted. You deserve to live the next part of your life victoriously. You deserve to live apart from the ghosts of the past. You can thrive despite the challenges that you have faced. Forgive and begin your journey that your heart may be restored.

APPENDIX

Self-Affirming Scriptures

Genesis 1:26 And God said, "Let us make mankind in our image, after our likeness, and let them have dominion over the fish of the sea, and over the fowl of the air, and over the cattle, and over all the earth, and over every creeping thing that creepeth upon the earth.

Psalm 139:14 I will praise thee; for I am fearfully and wonderfully made: marvelous are thy works; and that my soul knoweth right well.

Isaiah 64:8 But now, O Lord, thou art our father, we are the clay, and thou our potter; and we all are the work of thy hand.

2 Corinthians 3:18 But we all, with open face beholding as in a glass the glory of the Lord, are changed into the same image from glory to glory, even as by the Spirit of the Lord.

1 Peter 2:9 But ye are a chosen generation, a royal priesthood, an holy nation, a peculiar people; that ye should shew forth the praises of him who hath called you out of darkness into his marvelous light:

1 Peter 5:7 Casting all your care upon him; for he careth for you.

Romans 5:8 But God commendeth his love toward us, in that, while we were yet sinners, Christ died for us.

FORGIVENESS

John 15:15-16 Henceforth I call you not servants; for the servant knoweth not what his lord doeth: but I have called you friends; for all things that I have heard of my Father I have made known unto you.

1 Corinthians 6:20 For ye are bought with a price: therefore glorify God in your body, and in your spirit, which are God's.

Luke 12:7 But even the very hairs of your head are all numbered. Fear not therefore: ye are of more value than many sparrows.

Ephesians 2:10 For we are his workmanship, created in Christ Jesus unto good works, which God hath before ordained that we should walk in them.

Jeremiah 29:11 For I know the thoughts that I think toward you, saith the Lord, thoughts of peace, and not of evil, to give you an expected end.

MEET THE AUTHOR

Sharetta Donalson

Sharetta Donalson is an admired mentor to women from various walks of life. Her wisdom and advice is birthed through her many life's challenges coupled with the Word of God. She is now an author of her debut book, Forgiveness: The Quest for Healing Your Heart. In this book, she explains the life challenges that she encountered and overcame.

Just as she was enjoying the comfort of life as a Canton, MS Wife, Mother of 5, Grandmother of 1, and Registered Nurse in corporate America, she felt a tugging on her heart to come out of the closet as a sexual abuse survivor. Reluctantly, she began a journey to teach other survivors to come out, seek healing, and to forgive

Learn more or contact Sharetta at

www.forward-speaking.com

Facebook: Forward Speaking with Sharetta

Instagram: Forward Speaking